HORRID HENRY

MIDSUMMER MADNESS

FRANCESCA SIMON

FRANCESCA SIMON SPENT HER CHILDHOOD ON THE BEACH IN CALIFORNIA AND STARTED WRITING STORIES AT THE AGE OF EIGHT. SHE WROTE HER FIRST HORRID HENRY BOOK IN 1994. HORRID HENRY HAS GONE ON TO CONQUER THE GLOBE; HIS ADVENTURES HAVE SOLD MILLIONS OF COPIES WORLDWIDE.

FRANCESCA HAS WON THE CHILDREN'S BOOK OF THE YEAR AWARD AND IN 2009 WAS AWARDED A GOLD BLUE PETER BADGE. SHE WAS ALSO A TRUSTEE OF THE WORLD BOOK DAY CHARITY FOR SIX YEARS.

FRANCESCA LIVES IN NORTH LONDON WITH HER FAMILY.

WWW.FRANCESCASIMON.COM WWW.HORRIDHENRY.CO.UK @SIMON_FRANCESCA

TONY ROSS

TONY ROSS WAS BORN IN LONDON AND STUDIED AT THE LIVERPOOL SCHOOL OF ART AND DESIGN. HE HAS WORKED AS A CARTOONIST, A GRAPHIC DESIGNER, AN ADVERTISING ART DIRECTOR AND A UNIVERSITY LECTURER.

TONY IS ONE OF THE MOST POPULAR AND SUCCESSFUL CHILDREN'S ILLUSTRATORS OF ALL TIME, BEST KNOWN FOR ILLUSTRATING HORRID HENRY AND THE WORKS OF DAVID WALLIAMS, AS WELL AS HIS OWN HUGELY POPULAR SERIES, THE LITTLE PRINCESS. HE LIVES IN MACCLESFIELD.

HORRID HENRY

MiDSUMMER MADNESS

FRANCESCA SIMON
ILLUSTRATED BY TONY ROSS

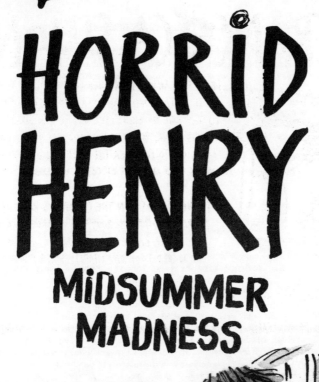

Orion

ORION CHILDREN'S BOOKS

Stories first published in "Horrid Henry Up, Up and Away",
"Horrid Henry's Nightmare", "Horrid Henry and the Abominable Snowman",
"Horrid Henry's Cannibal Curse", "Horrid Henry's Krazy Ketchup", and
"Horrid Henry Robs the Bank" respectively.

This collection first published in Great Britain in 2020 by Hodder and Stoughton

1 3 5 7 9 10 8 6 4 2

ISBN 978 1 5101 0715 1

Printed and bound in Great Britain by Clays Ltd, Elcograf S.p.A.

The paper and board used in this book are from well-managed forests and
other responsible sources.

MIX
Paper from
responsible sources
FSC® C104740
www.fsc.org

Orion Children's Books
An imprint of
Hachette Children's Group
Part of Hodder and Stoughton
Carmelite House
50 Victoria Embankment
London EC4Y 0DZ

An Hachette UK Company
www.hachette.co.uk

www.hachettechildrens.co.uk
www.horridhenry.co.uk

CONTENTS

HORRID HENRY
AND THE ZOOM OF DOOM

BOB BOB BOB BOB BOB.

The giant teacups bobbed down the lazy river.

"*Wheeeeeeee*," squealed Perfect Peter.

"*Wheeeeeeee*," squealed Tidy Ted.

"*Wheeeeeeee*," squealed Perky Parveen.

"*Wheeeeeeee!*" squealed all the mini ninnies seated in the giant floating teacups.

~~TERRIFIED SCREAMS~~ rang out from a nearby ride. Moody Margaret and Sour Susan and Brainy Brian and Jazzy Jim were *whizzing* down **Belly Flop Drop** in a **bouncing** rubber raft

9

which twisted and looped and spun
backwards.

"**DUCK**," hissed Henry. "Don't let them
see us."

Horrid Henry and RUDE RALPH
slunk down in their little seats as
low as they could. If Margaret or any
of their classmates saw them riding
in the *toddler teacups*, their names would

be **MUD** for ever.

"Sit up, Henry," said Miss Battle-Axe. "You too, Ralph."

Horrid Henry groaned.

How had he, Horrid Henry, ended up trapped in a giant teacup with **MISS BATTLE-AXE** and his *wormy worm* brother and the rest of *Miss Lovely's* infant class at **WILD WATER-SLIDE PARK**? He wanted to go racing down the **ZOOM OF DOOM**, the *TWISTING*, *LOOPING*, rollercoaster water slide with the world's **STEEPEST** drop. Where cannonballs blasted you as you hurtled backwards through waterfalls, flipping you upside down and spinning you as you crashed **SCREAMING** into Crocodile Creek. Or **Belly Flop Drop**, with its jet sprays and stomach-churning twists. Or **CRASH SPLASH**, where rubber rings raced towards each other before veering off into **TUNNELS OF TERROR**.

The shame. The misery. The horror of being trapped in giant *teacups* instead. With – oh **WOE** – only more *baby* rides to come.

It was so unfair. He'd worked his **fingers** to the **bone** earning all those badges.

Was it his fault he'd disappeared with **RUDE RALPH** on the last class trip? The class had got lost, not them. Or that he'd jumped from the little white train **chugging** around the Second World War airfield on the school trip before that, because he'd seen a plane he needed to investigate?

That certainly wasn't his fault — it was the school's, for not showing them anything interesting.

"Gondola ride on the Baby Bayou next, everyone," smiled *Miss Lovely*.

"*Yay*," trilled the infants.

"The gondolas are *so exciting*," said Goody-Goody Gordon.

"I don't want to go on the stupid gondola ride!" yelled Horrid Henry. "I want to go on the **ZOOM OF DOOM!!**"

"That's much too scary," said Perfect Peter.

"It's a straight drop to the bottom," GASPED Tidy Ted.

"I'm scared of heights," whimpered Perky Parveen.

"Don't worry, we won't be going anywhere near the **ZOOM OF DOOM**," said *Miss Lovely*.

"I want to go on the **ZOOM OF DOOM!**" howled Horrid Henry.

"Henry. Ralph. You're staying with me," said **MISS BATTLE-AXE**. "And that's final. There will be no repeat of last year. Or the year before that. And as I **DO NOT LIKE** water slides, we will be

15

sticking with *Miss Lovely's* class."

"**NOOOOOOOOOOOOO!**" howled
Horrid Henry.

"**NOOOOOOOOOOOOO!**" howled Rude
Ralph.

"**YES**," snapped **MISS BATTLE-AXE.**
She shuddered. VGGHH. She would
rather swim with **SHARKS** than
go on a water slide and be hurled
backwards into an abyss. The very
thought made her feel faint. Once
when she was a little girl she'd tried
a *teeny weeny* rollercoaster and spent a
week recovering from the fright in

a darkened
room. No water
slides for her.

Horrid Henry scowled. He had
to escape from Miss Battle-Axe and
get on the **ZOOM OF DOOM**. He had
to. He loved **scary rides** and **BIG
DROPS** and **ROLLERCOASTERS**
more than ANYTHING in the whole wide
world. The *TWISTIER*, the **TURNIER**,
the more *terrifying* the better. And
– oh, the AGONY – here he was, finally,
at **WILD WATER-SLIDE PARK**, and he
was trapped with the infants.

He whispered to **RUDE RALPH**.

Ralph smiled.

"Good plan," he said.

Just as their giant teacup reached the dock, **RUDE RALPH** stood up, *wobbled* and *toppled* over the side into the river. He started **splashing** and **SHRIEKING.**

"Man overboard!" shouted Horrid

Henry. "**HELP! HELP!**" He'd escape in all the commotion and get straight on the **ZOOM OF DOOM** before anyone could stop him.

Henry leapt off the teacup.

A *hideous* hand grabbed his shoulder.

"Not so fast," said **MISS BATTLE-AXE.**

"Why aren't you rescuing Ralph?" screamed Henry. "He's drowning."

"**HELP!**" yelped Ralph, **SPLUTTERING** and **FLAILING**. "**HELP!**"

"Stand up, Ralph," said **MISS BATTLE-AXE**. "Now."

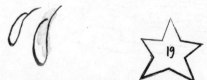

Slowly, **RUDE RALPH** stood up in the shallow water, which only reached his knees.

RATS.

"Everyone get in line and follow me to the Baby Bayou," trilled *Miss Lovely*.

"Yay," said Perfect Peter. "The Baby Bayou is my favourite ride."

Horrid Henry pinched Peter.

Perfect Peter screamed.

"Henry pinched me!" he wailed.

"I was just checking to see if you were an *alien*," *hissed* Henry. "And you are."

Moody Margaret and Sour Susan strolled past, laughing.

"Oh wow, that was so much fun," *squealed* Moody Margaret.

"Yeah," *squealed* Sour Susan.

"Let's go on the **ZOOM OF DOOM** now," said Margaret loudly. "And then **Belly Flop Drop** again."

"Yeah," said Sour Susan.

"Did you enjoy the giant teacups, Henry? I hope you weren't too scared," said Moody Margaret, smirking.

Horrid Henry gritted his teeth.

What could he say? Or do? Other than hope that a **GIANT SEA MONSTER** would rise up from the Lazy River and swallow Margaret whole.

"Too bad you won't get to ride the **ZOOM OF DOOM**, Henry," said Margaret.

"**NAH NAH NE NAH NAH**," jeered Margaret and Susan, racing off to join the long queue snaking away from the entrance to the **ZOOM OF DOOM**.

"We've got to escape," muttered Horrid Henry.

"Too right," said **RUDE RALPH**.

Henry looked at Ralph.

Ralph looked at Henry.

"Run!" shouted **Horrid Henry**.

Henry and Ralph ran off as fast as they could. They darted through the crowds, *pushing* and **shoving** and LEAPING, closer and closer to the

ZOOM OF D—

CRASH! BANG!

"And where do you think you're going?" came a TERRIBLE voice.

Huh?

There was **MISS BATTLE-AXE** standing in front of them, arms crossed. They'd slammed right into her.

"We needed the loo," said Henry.

"It was an emergency," said RUDE RALPH.

MISS BATTLE-AXE glared at them.

"If you so much as move an INCH from my side again, you will be taken straight to the BAD CHILDREN'S ROOM to wait for your parents to collect you," said Miss Battle-Axe.

Yikes.

THE BAD CHILDREN'S ROOM.

If Henry got sent home he'd have NO chance of ever getting on the ZOOM OF DOOM. His parents would never take him back to WILD

WATER-SLIDE PARK, that was for sure.

He'd have to grit his teeth and find another way.

Horrid Henry and Rude Ralph followed the infants to the gondolas on the Baby Bayou.

"I feel **SEASICK**," said **RUDE RALPH** suddenly. "Those teacups made me dizzy. I need to go to the First Aid room." He **belched** loudly, then **WINKED** at Henry.

"**ohhhh!** Yeah, me too," said Horrid Henry. He clutched his stomach. "**OWW. OWWWW.** You can just leave us to recover there," he moaned. "We don't want to stop anyone having fun."

Miss Battle-Axe took **Horrid Henry** and **RUDE RALPH**, groaning and moaning, to the First Aid room.

They lay down on two cots.

"No need to stay with us," **GROANED** Henry.

"We'll just lie here till it's home time," **MOANED** Ralph.

"These boys are suffering from seasickness," said **MISS BATTLE-AXE** to the nurse.

"Tummy ache?" said the nurse.

"Yes," moaned Henry.

"Dizzy?"

"Oh yes," said Ralph.

"Feeling like you are going to vomit?"

"Any second," said Henry.

"Not to worry," said the nurse.

"I have just the right injection." She advanced towards them, waving two ENORMOUS needles.

"You know, I feel a lot better," said Henry, sitting up.

"Me too," said Ralph.

"Excellent," said **MISS BATTLE-AXE**. "Now off we go to the **Dozy Dinghies**. If we're lucky, we'll catch *Miss Lovely* at the steamboats for a relaxing journey around the Pixie Pond."

How was it possible, thought Henry miserably, trudging after her, to have so many baby rides in a water-slide park?

He could see Tough Toby and Fiery Fiona whizzing down **PANIC PRECIPICE**, whooping and laughing while he was trapped on the *Pixie Pond*.

"Last ride before home time," said *Miss Lovely*. "*Lullaby Lagoon* or the *Fairy Float Boats*?"

"*Lullaby Lagoon* might be too scary," said Spotless Sam.

"How about the **CANNIBAL CANOES**, where you get eaten as you ride?" snarled **Horrid Henry**. "That's why all the canoes come back empty."

"Quiet, Henry," said **MISS BATTLE-AXE**. Soon, she'd be safely home, with her feet up, and the school outing would

30

be over for another year.

"*Fairy Floats, Fairy Floats*," chanted the infants.

"Where are the *Fairy Float Boats*?" said *Miss Lovely*. Miss Battle-Axe consulted her map.

"Right next to the **ZOOM OF DOOM**," said **MISS BATTLE-AXE**, pointing to the huge queues jostling each other waiting for both rides.

Just to torture him, thought **Horrid Henry** as he plodded over to the queue for the *Fairy Float Boats*. Could his day have got even worse?

So near, and yet so far.

There were so many people *pushing* and **SHOVING** that the queues were starting to mix. You couldn't tell which queue was which.

And then Horrid Henry had a brilliant, **SPECTACULAR** idea. It was *perilous.* It was **DANGEROUS.** The chance of success was tiny. And yet . . . and yet . . . how could he not risk his life for a chance to ride the **ZOOM OF DOOM**?

"Come on, everyone, this way, this way," said Henry, weaving through

the **MASSIVE** queues. Perfect Peter, Goody-Goody Gordon and Tidy Ted followed him.

Slowly, Henry *inched* his way to the right, into the **ZOOM OF DOOM** queue.

"Follow me," shouted RUDE RALPH, ushering **MISS BATTLE-AXE**, *Miss Lovely* and her class to the right, behind Henry.

Finally they reached the head of the queue.

"What's this ride again?" asked Perky Parveen.

"*Fairy Float Boats*," said Henry,

grabbing a seat at the front of the **BLACK SKULL** raft.

"Oh, I love the Fairy Float Boats," said Perfect Peter.

Miss Lovely and **MISS BATTLE-AXE** sat down.

"I don't remember seat belts on the Fairy Float Boats," said Miss Battle-Axe, buckling up. "Do you, Lydia?"

"No," said Miss Lovely. "Must be new HEALTH AND SAFETY rules. Seat belts on, everyone."

The rubber rafts began a slow ascent up the track.

"Lydia," said Miss Battle-Axe. "I don't remember riding in **BLACK SKULLS** on the *Fairy Float Boats*, do you?"

"Must be a new design," said Miss Lovely.

The rafts climbed higher. Soft music began to play.

"Boudicca," said *Miss Lovely*, "don't we seem rather high up for the *Fairy Float Boats* . . ."

"Now that you mention it," said Miss Battle-Axe. She peered over the edge. "Lydia, I've got the feeling we're not—"

But before she could finish speaking

the raft PLUNGED over the edge, SPUN BACKWARDS and **PLUMMETED** straight down.

MISS BATTLE-AXE screamed.

"AAAAARRRGGGGHHHIIE"

Miss Lovely screamed.

The infants screamed.

"WHOOPEEEEE!" shrieked Henry and Ralph. They'd done it. They were riding on the ZOOM OF DOOM at last.

Life was sweet.

FLuFFy

STRUTS HER STUFF

"Fluffy. Fetch," said Perfect Peter.

SNORE.

"Fluffy. Fetch!" said Perfect Peter.

SNORE.

"Go on, Fluffy," said Perfect Peter, dangling a squeaky toy TARANTULA in front of the snoozing cat. "Fetch!"

FAT FLUFFY stretched.

Yawn.

SNORE. SNORE.

"What are you doing, *worm?*" said Horrid Henry.

Peter jumped. Should he tell

Henry about his brilliant idea? What
if Henry copied him? That would
be just like Henry. Well, let him try,
thought Peter. FLUFFY is my cat.

"I'm training Fluffy for SCRUFFS," said
Peter. "She's sure to WIN this year."

Scruffs was the
annual neighbourhood
pet show. Last year
Henry had spent one of
the most boring days
of his life
watching HORRIBLE
dogs compete for who

looked the most like their
owner, or who had
the *waggiest* tail or
FLUFFIEST coat.
Horrid Henry snorted.
"Which category?" said
Henry. "Ugliest Owner?
FATTEST Cat?"
"Most Obedient," said
Peter.
Horrid Henry
snorted again.
Trust his *worm
toad nappy face*

43

brother to come up with such a
dumb idea.

FAT FLUFFY was the world's
most useless cat. Fluffy did
nothing but eat and sleep
and **SNORE**. She was so
lazy that Horrid Henry was
shocked every time she moved.

Squeak! Perfect Peter waved the
rubber TARANTULA in front of Fluffy's
face. He knew Henry would make
fun of him. Well, this time he, Peter,
would have the
last laugh. He

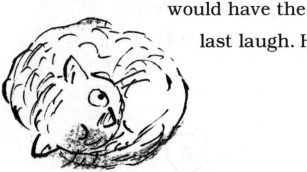

would show the world what an **AMAZING** cat Fluffy was, and no one, especially Henry, could stop him. Peter knew that **FLUFFY** had hidden greatness. After all, thought Peter, not everyone knows how clever I am. The same was true of Fluffy.

"Fluffy, when I squeak this toy, you sit up and give me your paw," said Peter. "When I squeak it twice, you roll over."

"You can't train a cat, *toad*," said Henry.

"Yes I can," said Peter. "And don't

call me toad." What did Henry know, anyway? Nothing. Peter had seen dogs herding sheep. Jumping through hoops. Even dancing.

True, they had all been dogs, and **FLUFFY** was a cat. But she was no ordinary cat.

Horrid Henry smirked.

"Okay, Peter, because I'm such a nice brother I'll show you how to *train* Fluffy," said Henry.

"Can you really?" said Peter.

"Yup," said Henry. "When I give the command, **FLUFFY** will do

exactly what I say."

So far that was more than Peter had managed. A lot more.

"And it will only cost you one pound," said Henry.

Well, it was definitely worth a pound if it meant Fluffy could win Most Obedient.

Peter handed over the money.

"Now watch and learn, **WORM**," said Horrid Henry. "Fluffy. Sleep!"

Fluffy slept.

"See?" said Henry. "She obeyed."

Perfect Peter was outraged.

"That doesn't count," said Peter. "I want my money back."

"You can't have it," said Henry. "I did exactly what I said I would do."

"Mum!" wailed Peter. "Henry tricked me."

"Shut up, toad," said Horrid Henry.

"Mum! Henry told me to shut up," screamed Peter.

"Henry! Don't be HORRID," shouted Mum.

Horrid Henry wasn't listening. He was an idiot. He had just had the most brilliant, SPECTACULAR idea. He could train Fluffy and play the best ever trick on Peter in the history of the world. No, the universe. That would pay Peter back for getting Henry into such **BIG TROUBLE** over breaking Mum's camera. One day, thought Horrid Henry, he would write a famous book collecting all his best tricks, and sell it for a *million pounds* a copy. *Parliament* would declare a special holiday — Henry Day — to celebrate his brilliance. There would be street parties and parades in his honour. The Queen would knight him. But until then . . .

he had work to do.

Horrid Henry gave Peter back his £1 coin.

Perfect Peter was amazed.

Henry never handed back money voluntarily. He looked at the coin suspiciously. Had Henry substituted a plastic pound coin like the last time?

"That was just a joke," said Henry smoothly. "Of course I can train FLUFFY for you."

"How?" said Peter. He'd been trying for days.

"That's my secret," said Henry. "But I am so confident I can do it I'll even give you a **money-back guarantee**."

A money-back guarantee! That sounded almost too good to be true.

In fact . . .

"Is this a trick?" said Peter.

"No!" said Henry. "Out of the goodness of my heart, I offer to spend my valuable time training your cat. I'm insulted. Just for that I won't—"

"Okay," said Peter. "How much?"

Yes! thought Horrid Henry.

"Five pounds," said Henry.

"Five pounds!" gasped Peter.

"That's a bargain," said Henry. "Not everyone can train a cat. Okay, five pounds money-back guarantee that FLUFFY will obey four commands in

52

time for Scruffs. If not, you'll get
your money back."

How could I lose? thought Peter.

"Deal," he said.

Yes! thought Horrid Henry.

Somehow he didn't think he'd have
too much trouble
training FLUFFY
to **STAY**. SLEEP.
Breathe. **SNORE**. No
trouble at all.

Perfect Peter **bounced** up and down with excitement. Today was the big day. Today was the day when he took FLUFFY to win Most Obedient pet at Scruffs.

"Shouldn't I practise with her?" said Peter.

"No!" said Henry quickly. "Cats are tricky. You only get one chance to make them obey, so we need to save it for the judge."

"Okay, Henry," said Peter. After all, Henry had given him a **money-back guarantee**.

Greedy Graham was at the park with his **ENORMOUS** guinea pig, **Fattie**. Rude Ralph had brought his mutt, **WINDBAG**, who was competing for *Waggiest Tail*. Sour Susan was there with her pug, Grumpy. Aerobic Al was there with his greyhound,

Speedy. Lazy Linda's
rabbit, Snore, dozed
on her shoulder.
Even Miss
Lovely had brought her
Yorkie, Baby Jane. There
were pets everywhere.

"What's your dog called,
Bert?" said Henry.

"I dunno," said Beefy Bert.

"Waaah," wailed Weepy William. "Mr
Socks didn't win the 𝓕𝓁𝓾𝓯𝓯𝓲𝓮𝓼𝓽 𝓚𝓲𝓽𝓽𝔂
contest."

"Piddle. Sit!" came a familiar, steely

voice, like a jagged knife being dragged across a boulder.

Horrid Henry gasped.

There was **MISS BATTLE-AXE**, walking beside the most groomed dog Henry had ever seen. The poodle was covered in ribbons and fancy collars and *velvet bows*.

He watched as Miss Battle-Axe found a quiet corner and put on some music.

Boom-chick boom-chick boom-chick-boom!

MISS BATTLE-AXE danced around Piddle.

She clicked her fingers.

Piddle danced around Miss Battle-Axe.

Miss Battle-Axe danced backwards,

waving her arms and clicking again.

PIDDLE danced backwards.

Miss Battle-Axe danced forwards, hopping. Piddle danced forwards.

Double click. **MISS BATTLE-AXE** danced off to the left. PIDDLE danced off to the right. Then they met back at the centre.

Finally, Miss Battle-Axe crouched, and Piddle **jumped** over her.

"Wow," said Perfect Peter, glancing

at FAT FLUFFY snoring on the grass. "Do you think we could teach Fluffy to do tricks like that?"

"Already have," said Horrid Henry.

Peter gazed at Henry open-mouthed. "Really?" said Peter.

"Yup," said Henry. "Just squeeze the TARANTULA and tell Fluffy what you want her to do."

"Line up here for Most Obedient pet," said the organiser.

"That's me!" said Peter.

"All you have to remember is, one squeak to make FLUFFY sit

up, two squeaks to make her walk on her hind legs," said Henry as they stood in the queue. "Three squeaks will make her come running to you."

"Okay, Henry," said Peter.

Tee hee.

Revenge was **SWEET**, thought Horrid Henry. Wouldn't Peter look an **IDIOT** trying to give orders to a cat? And naturally he'd find a way to keep Peter's £5.

Peter handed in his entry ticket at the enclosure's entrance.

"Sorry, your brother's too young,"

said the man at the gate. "You'll have to show the cat."

Horrid Henry froze with horror.

"Me?" said Horrid Henry. "But . . . but . . ."

"But she's my cat," said Perfect Peter. "I—"

"Come along, come along, we're about to start," said the man, SHOVING Henry and FAT FLUFFY into the ring.

Horrid Henry found himself standing in the centre. He had the only cat. Everyone was STARING and

pointing and *laughing*. Oh, where was a cloak of invisibility when you needed one?

"Put your pets through their paces now," shouted the judge.

All the dogs started to Sit. Stay. Come. Fetch. PIDDLE the poodle began to dance.

Fluffy lay curled in a ball at Henry's feet.

"Stay!" said Horrid Henry as the judge walked by.

Maybe he could get FLUFFY at least to sit up. Or even just move a bit.

Horrid Henry squeezed the TARANTULA toy.

Squeak!

"Come on, Fluffy. Move!"

Fluffy didn't even raise her head.

SQUEAK! SQUEAK! SQUEAK!

"Fluffy. Wake up!"

Aerobic Al's dog began to bark.

Horrid Henry squeezed the TARANTULA
toy again.

SQUEAK! SQUEAK!

Piddle stood on his hind legs and
danced in a circle.

"No, Piddle," hissed Miss Battle-Axe,
gesturing wildly, "turn to the right."

"Fluffy. Sit!" said Horrid Henry.

SQUEAK! SQUEAK!

Babbling Bob's mutt started

GROWLING.

Come on, Fluffy, thought Horrid Henry desperately, squeezing the toy in front of the dozing cat. "Do something. Anything."

SQUEAK! SQUEAK! SQUEEEEEEEEAK!

Piddle ran over and peed on the judge's leg.

"Piddle," squawked Miss Battle-Axe.

"NO!"

SQUEAK! SQUEAK! SQUEAK!

66

Sour Susan's dog Grumpy bit the dog next to him.

Horrid Henry waved his arms. "Come on, FLUFFY. You can do it!"

Weepy William's dog started running in circles.

"Piddle! Come back!" shrieked **MISS BATTLE-AXE** as PIDDLE ran from the ring, howling. Every other dog chased after him, **barking** and *yelping*, their owners running after them SCREAMING.

The only animal left was FAT FLUFFY.

"Fluffy. Stay!" ordered Horrid
Henry.

SNORE. SNORE. SNORE.

"The cat's the **WINNER**," said
the judge.

"Yippee!" screamed
Perfect Peter.
"I knew you
could do
it, Fluffy!"

Horrid Henry was bored.
Horrid Henry was fed up.
He'd been **BANNED** from the computer
for rampaging through Our Town
Museum. He'd been **BANNED** from
watching TV just because he was
caught watching a TEENY TINY bit extra
after he'd been told to switch it off
straight after **Mutant Max**. Could
he help it if an exciting new series
about a rebel robot had started
right after? How would he know if
it were any good unless he watched
some of it?

It was completely unfair and all Peter's fault for telling on him, and Mum and Dad were the MEANEST, most horrible parents in the world.

And now he was stuck indoors, all day long, with absolutely NOTHING to do.

The rain splattered down. The house was grey. The world was grey. The universe was grey.

"I'M BORED!" wailed Horrid Henry.

"Read a book," said Mum.

"Do your homework," said Dad.

"**NO!**" said Horrid Henry.

"Then tidy your room," said Mum.

"Unload the dishwasher," said Dad.

"Empty the bins," said Mum.

"**NO WAY!**" shrieked Horrid Henry. What was he, a **SLAVE?** Better keep out of his parents' way, or they'd come up with even more **horrible** things for him to do.

Horrid Henry stomped up to his boring bedroom and *slammed* the door. **UGGH.** He **HATED** all his toys. He **HATED** all his music.

He **HATED** all his games.

UGGGHHHHHH!

What could he do?

Aha.

He could always check to see what Peter was up to.

Perfect Peter was sitting in his room arranging stamps in his stamp album.

"Peter is a baby, Peter is a baby," jeered **Horrid Henry**, sticking his head round the door.

"Don't call me baby," said Perfect Peter.

"Okay, **Duke of Poop**," said Henry.

"Don't call me **Duke**!" shrieked Peter.

"Okay, Poopsicle," said Henry.

"MUUUUM!" wailed Peter. "Henry called me Poopsicle!"

"Don't be **HORRID**, Henry!" shouted Mum. "Stop calling your brother names."

Horrid Henry smiled sweetly at Peter.

"Okay, Peter, 'cause I'm so nice, I'll let you make a list of ten names that you don't want to be called," said Henry. "And it will only cost you £1."

£1! Perfect Peter could not believe his ears. Peter would pay much more than that never to be called Poopsicle again.

"Is this a trick, Henry?" said Peter.

"No," said Henry. "How dare you? I make you a good offer, and you accuse me. Well, just for that—"

"Wait," said Peter. "I accept." He handed Henry a pound coin. At last, all those **HORRID** names would be banned. Henry would never call him

Duke of Poop again.

Peter got out a piece of paper and a pencil.

Now, let's see, what to put on the list? thought Peter. Poopsicle, for a start. And I hate being called Baby, and **Nappy Face**, and **Duke of Poop**.

Peter wrote and wrote and wrote.

"Okay, Henry, here's the list," said Peter.

NAMES I DON'T WANT TO BE CALLED
1. Poopsicle
2. Duke of Poop
3. Ugly
4. Nappy face
5. Baby
6 Toad
7. Smelly toad
8. Ugg
9. Worm
10. Wibble pants

Horrid Henry scanned the list.
"Fine, PONGY PANTS," said Henry.
"Sorry, I meant **poopy pants**. Or was it
SMELLY NAPPY?"

"MUUUMM!" wailed Peter. "Henry's
calling me names!"

"**HENRY!**" screamed Mum. "For the
last time, can't you leave your brother
alone?"

Horrid Henry considered. Could he
leave that *worm* alone?

"Peter
is a
frog,

Peter is a frog," chanted
Henry.

"MUUUUUMMMMM!" screamed Peter.

"That's it, Henry!" shouted Mum.
"No **POCKET MONEY** for a week. Go
to your room and stay there."

"**FINE!**" shrieked Henry. "You'll
all be sorry when I'm **DEAD**." He
stomped down the hall and *slammed*
his bedroom door as hard as he
could. Why were his parents so *mean*
and **HORRIBLE**? He was hardly
bothering Peter at all. Peter **WAS** a
frog. Henry was only telling the truth.

Boy, would they be sorry
when he'd died of boredom
stuck up here.

If only we'd let
him watch a little
extra TV, Mum
would wail. Would

that have been so

TERRIBLE?

If only we hadn't
made him do any
chores, Dad would
sob.

Why didn't I let

Henry call me names, Peter would howl. After all, I do have **smelly pants**.

And now it's too late and we're **Sooooooo SORRY**, they would shriek.

But wait. Would they be sorry? Peter would *grab* his room. And all his best toys. His arch-enemy **STUCK-UP STEVE** could come over and snatch anything he wanted, even his **skeleton bank** and **Goo-Shooter**. Peter could invade the **PURPLE HAND FORT** and Henry couldn't stop him. Moody Margaret could hop over the wall and nick his flag. And his **biscuits**.

And his Dungeon Drink Kit. Even his . . .
SUPERSOAKER.

NOOOOOO!!!

Horrid Henry went pale. He had
to stop those rapacious thieves.
But how?

I could come back and **haunt** them,

thought Horrid Henry. Yes! That
would teach those grave-robbers
not to mess with me.

"**oooooooo, get out of
my rooooooooooom,
you horrrrrrrible
toooooooooooad**," he would
moan at Peter.

"Touch my **Gooooooooo-shooooooter** and
you'll be *morphed* into **ectoplasm**," he'd
groan spookily from under STUCK-UP
STEVE'S bed. Ha! That would show him.

Or he'd pop out from inside MOODY
MARGARET'S wardrobe.

"Giiiiive Henrrrrry's toyyyys back, you mis-er-a-ble sliiiiiimy snake," he would rasp. That would teach her a thing or two.

Henry smiled. But fun as it would be to haunt people, he'd rather stop horrible enemies **SNATCHING** his stuff in the first place.

And then suddenly **Horrid Henry**

had a brilliant, SPECTACULAR idea. Hadn't Mum told him just the other day that people wrote wills to say who they wanted to get all their stuff when they died? Henry had been thrilled.

"So when you die I get all your money!" Henry beamed. WOW. The HOUSE would be his! And the CAR! And he'd be boss of the TV, 'cause it would be his, too! And the only shame was—

"Couldn't you just give it all to me now?" asked Henry.

"**HENRY!**" snapped Mum. "Don't be **HORRID**."

There was no time to lose. He had to write a will immediately.

Horrid Henry sat down at his desk and grabbed some paper.

MY WILL
WARNING: DO NOT READ UNLESS
I AM DEAD!!!! I mean it!!!!

If you're reading this it's because I'm dead and you aren't. I wish you were dead and I wasn't, so I could have all your stuff. It's so not fair.

First of all, to anyone thinking of snatching my stuff just 'cause I'm dead ...

BEWARE! Anyone who doesn't do what I say will get haunted by a bloodless and boneless ghoul, namely me. So there.

Now the hard bit, thought Horrid Henry. Who should get his things? Was anyone deserving enough?

Peter, you are a worm. And a toad. And an ugly baby nappy face smelly ugg wibble pants poopsicle. I leave you ...

Hmmmn.

That **toad** really shouldn't get anything. But Peter was his brother after all.

I leave you my sweet wrappers.

And a muddy twig.

That was more than Peter deserved. Still . . .

Steve, you are stuck-up and horrible and the world's worst cousin. You can have a pair of my socks. You can choose the blue ones with the holes or the falling down orange ones.

Margaret, you nit-face. I give you the Purple

Hand flag to remember me by— NOT! You can have two radishes and the knight with the chopped-off head. And keep your paws off my Grisly Grub Box!!! Or else . . .

Miss Battle-Axe, you are my worst teacher ever. I leave you a broken pencil.

Aunt Ruby, you can have the lime green cardigan back that you gave me for Christmas.

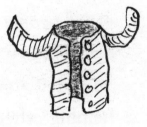

Hmmm. So far he wasn't doing so well giving away any of his good things.

Ralph, you can have my Goo-Shooter, but ONLY if you give me your football and your bike and your computer game Slime Ghouls.

That was more like it. After all, why should he be the only one writing a will? It was certainly a lot more fun thinking about getting stuff from other people than giving away his own treasures.

In fact, wouldn't he be better off helping others by telling them what he wanted? Wouldn't it be AWFUL if Rich Aunt Ruby left him some of Steve's old clothes in her will thinking

that he would be delighted? Better
write to her at once.

Dear Aunt Ruby
I am leeving you
Something ~~greet REELy~~
~~GREAT~~ REELY
REELY GREAT in
my will, so make sure
you leeve no loads of
Cash in yours.
    Your favorite nephew
        Henry

Now, Steve. Henry was leaving him an **old pair of holey socks**. But Steve didn't have to know that, did he. For all Henry knew, Steve **LOVED** holey socks.

Dear Steve

You know your new blue racing bike with the silver trim? Well when your dead. it wont be any use to you, so please leave it to me in your will

Your favourite cousin
Henry

P.S By the way, no need to wait 'till your dead, you can give it to me now.

Right, Mum and Dad. When they were in the old people's home they'd hardly need a thing. A *rocking chair* and *blanket* each would do fine for them.

So, how would Dad's *music system* look in his bedroom? And where could he put Mum's **CLOCK RADIO**? Henry had always liked the *chiming* *clock* on their mantelpiece and the picture of the blackbird. Better go and check to see where he could put them.

Henry went into Mum and Dad's room, and *grabbed* an armload of stuff. He **staggered** to his bedroom and **DUMPED** everything

on the floor,
then went back
for a second
helping.
stumbling
and **staggering**

under his heavy burden, Horrid
Henry *swayed* down the hall and
CRASHED into Dad.

"What are you doing?" said Dad,
staring. "That's mine."

"And those are mine," said Mum.
"**WHAT IS GOING ON?**" shrieked
Mum and Dad.

"I was just checking how all this
stuff will look in my room when
you're in the old people's home,"
said **Horrid Henry**.

"I'm not there yet," said Mum.

"Put **EVERYTHING** back," said Dad.

Horrid Henry **SCOWLED**. Here he

was, just trying to think ahead, and he got told off.

"Well, just for that I **WON'T** leave you **ANY** of my knights in my will," said Henry.

Honestly, some people were so selfish.

HORRID HENRY'S

BAKE-OFF

THWACK!
THWACK!
THWACK!

Moody Margaret thwacked the wall with a stick.

Why oh why did she have to live next door to someone as **HORRID** as Henry?

Her club wasn't safe. Her biscuits weren't safe. And he was such a COPY-CAT. She'd told everyone she was making a **chocolate** sponge cake for the street party bake-off competition,

and now Henry was saying he was making a **chocolate** sponge cake. And pretending he'd thought of it first.

Well, she'd show him. Her cake was sure to WIN. For once she'd have the last laugh.

Although . . .

Hmmm . . .

Maybe she could make sure of that . . .

A street party bake-off! Hurrah!

Horrid Henry loved baking. What

could be better than choosing exactly
what you wanted to eat and then
cooking it exactly as you liked it?
With **LOADS** of extra *sugar* and lashings
of *icing*?

Horrid Henry loved making *fudge*.
Horrid Henry loved making *brownies*.
Horrid Henry loved baking *chocolate*
cakes.

His parents, unfortunately, only
liked him to make **HORRIBLE** food.
Pizzas ruined with vegetable toppings.
Sloppy *gloppy* porridge. And if they
ever let him make muffins, they

had to be wholesome muffins. With wholemeal flour. And bananas.

UGGGH.

But today, no one could stop him. It was a cake baking contest. And what a cake he'd make. His **chocolate** sponge cake with extra icing was guaranteed to win. He'd heard that copy-cat Margaret was making one too. Let old **FROG FACE** try. No one could out-bake Chef Henry.

Plus, the **WINNER** would get their picture in the paper, AND be on TV, because the famous pastry chef

Cherry Berry was coming to judge. **Whoopee!**

Everyone in Henry's class was taking part.

Too bad, losers, thought **Horrid Henry**, dashing to the kitchen. Chef Henry is in the room.

Unfortunately, someone else was too.

Perfect Peter was wearing a Daffy Daisy apron and peering anxiously at the oven while Mum took out a baking tray laden with mysterious grey **globs**.

"Out of my way, **worm**," said Henry.

"I've made cupcakes for the bake-off," said Peter. "Look."

Perfect Peter proudly pointed to the plate covered in LUMPY blobs. His name was written on a flag poking out of one cupcake.

"Those aren't cupcakes," said Henry. "They're lopsided cowpats."

"Mum," wailed Peter. "Henry called my cupcakes cowpats."

"Don't be **HORRID**, Henry," said Mum. "Peter, I think your cupcakes look — lovely."

PLOPCAKES more like," said Henry.

"MUM!" screamed Peter. "Henry said plopcakes."

"Stop it, Henry," said Mum.

Tee hee.

All the better for him. No need to worry about Peter's SAGGY disasters winning.

His real competition was Margaret.

Henry hated to admit it, but she was almost as good a chef as he was. Well, no way was she beating him today. Her copy-cat **chocolate** sponge cake wouldn't be a patch on his.

"Henry. Peter. Come out and help hang up the bunting and get cloths on the tables," said Dad. "The street party starts at two o'clock."

"But I have to bake my cake," yelped Henry, weighing the *sugar* and **chocolate**. He always put in extra.

"There's plenty of time," said Mum. "But I need you to help me now."

MOODY MARGARET sneaked through the back door into Henry's kitchen. She'd waited until she'd seen Henry and his family go outside to help set up the tables.

If she was too late and his cake was already baking, she could open the oven door and **stomp** to make Henry's sponge COLLAPSE.

Or she could turn the temperature way up high, or *scoop* out the middle, or—

Margaret sniffed.

She couldn't smell anything baking.

What a bit of luck.

There were all Henry's ingredients on the counter, measured out and waiting to be used.

Snatch!

MOODY MARGARET grabbed the sugar jar and emptied it into the bin. Then she re-filled it with salt.

Tee hee, thought MOODY MARGARET.

Wouldn't it be
wonderful to pay Henry back?

"What are you doing here?" came a
little voice.

Oops.

MOODY MARGARET whirled round.

"What are you doing here?" said
Margaret.

"I live here," said Peter.

"I must have come into the wrong
house," said Margaret. "How silly of me."

"Out of my way, **worm**," came Henry's
HORRIBLE voice as he slammed the
front door.

"Byeeee," said Margaret, as she skedaddled out of the back door.

Phew.

Revenge was *sweet*, she thought happily. Or in this case, salty.

Should he tell Henry that Margaret had come over? No, thought Peter. Henry called my cupcakes **PLOPCAKES**.

Horrid Henry proudly stuck his name flag in his **FABULOUS** cake.

What a triumph.

His glorious **chocolate** sponge, drowning in **LUSCIOUS** icing, was definitely his best ever.

He was sure to win. He was absolutely sure to win. Just wait till *Cherry Berry* tried a mouthful of his cake. He'd be offered his own TV baking programme. He'd write his own cookbook. But instead of **HORRIBLE** recipes like 10 ways to cook broccoli — as if that would make any difference to how **YUCKY** it was — he'd have recipes for things kids actually liked to eat instead of what

their parents wanted them to eat.

Chips,

Chocolate worms,

FROSTY FREEZE ICE-CREAM,

VEG-FREE CHEESE PIZZA.

He'd write:

"Take wrapping off pizza. Put in oven. Or, if you are feeling lazy, ring Pizza Delivery to skip the boring unwrapping and putting in oven bit."

Yes! He'd add a few recipes with **ketchup**, then sit back and count the **DOUGH**.

Horrid Henry sighed happily. Didn't that icing look **YUMMALICIOUS**. He'd left loads in the bowl, and more on the spoon. Oh boy, *chocolate* here I come, thought Horrid Henry. Chefs always taste their own food, don't they, he thought, shoving a huge succulent spoonful into his mouth and—

BLECCCCCHHHHHH.

YUCK.

AAAARRRRGGGGH!

Horrid Henry gagged.

Ugh.

He spat it out, gasping and choking.

UGH.

It tasted worse than anything

he'd ever tasted in his life. It was

HORRIBLE. **Disgusting**. Revolting.

Worse than sprouts.

So bitter. So salty.

Horrid Henry choked down some

water.

How was it possible? What could he

have done?

He'd been so careful, measuring out the ingredients. How could a teaspoon of salt have got into his icing?

But this wasn't even a TEASPOON.

This was a bucket load.

There was only one explanation . . .

Sabotage.

Peter must have done it, in revenge for Henry calling his cupcakes cowpats.

Wait till I get my hands on you, Peter, you'll be sorry, you *wormy worm toad—*

Wait.

Horrid Henry paused.

Was Perfect Peter evil enough to have come up with such a dastardly plan?

No.

Was he clever enough?

No.

It had to be someone so **vile**, so sly, so despicable, they would **sabotage** a cake.

There was only one person he knew who fitted that description.

MARGARET.

Well, he'd show her.

ROOT A TOOT!
ROOT A TOOT!
ROOT A TOOT TOOT TOOT!

Margaret was blasting away on her trumpet. Blasting what she thought was a victory tune.

Not this time, frog face, thought **Horrid Henry**, sneaking into **MOODY MARGARET'S** kitchen.

There was her *chocolate* sponge cake, resting proudly on a *flowery* china stand. What luck she'd copied him.

Whisk!

Henry snatched Margaret's cake.

Switch!

Henry plopped his salt cake on the cake stand instead.

Swap!

He stuck the name flag "Margaret" into his old cake.

Then he sneaked back home, clutching his stolen one.

Horrid Henry placed his name flag in Margaret's cake and stood back.

He had to admit, Margaret's cake was GORGEOUS. So chocolatey. So springy. So much **chocolate** icing whirling and swirling in thick globs.

Margaret was a moody old grouch, but she certainly knew how to bake a cake.

It looked good enough to eat.

And then suddenly Horrid Henry had a **HORRIBLE** thought.

What if Margaret had baked a decoy cake, made with soap powder instead of flour, and left it out to tempt him to steal it? Margaret was so evil, it would be just like her to come up with such a cunning plan.

Don't let her fool you twice, screeched Henry's tummy.

He'd better take the TEENSIEST bite, just to make sure. He'd cover up the hole with icing, no problem.

Horrid Henry took a tiny bite

from the back.

Oh my.

Chocolate heaven.

This cake was great.

WOW.

But what if she'd put some bad bits in the middle? He'd better take another small bite just to check. He wouldn't want *Cherry Berry* to be poisoned, would he?

CHOMP
CHOMP
CHOMP

Horrid Henry stopped chewing.
Where had that **huge** hole in the
cake come from? He couldn't have—
YIKES.

What was he thinking?

There was only one thing to do. He
had to fill the hole fast. If he covered
it with icing no one would ever know.

What could he fill the cake with to
disguise the missing piece?

Newspaper?

Nah. Too bumpy.

Rice?

Too bitty.

Horrid Henry looked wildly around the kitchen.

Aha.

A SPONGE. A sponge for a sponge cake.

He was a *genius*.

Quickly Horrid Henry cut the sponge to fit the hole, slipped it inside, and covered the joins with more icing.

Perfect.

No one would ever know.

Mum came into the kitchen.

"Hurry up, Henry, and bring your
cake out. It's street party time."

Horrid Henry had a brilliant time
at the street party. Everyone was
there. Magic Martha did magic tricks
in the corner. Jazzy Jim banged on
his keyboard. Singing
Soraya warbled behind
the bouncy castle.
Jolly Josh showed off his
tap dancing.

Even Margaret playing solo trumpet and Perfect Peter singing with his band, The Golden Goodies, couldn't ruin Henry's mood. He'd eyed the other contestants as they carried their entries to the bake-off table. Rude Ralph had brought burnt brownies. Sour Susan had made **HORRIBLE**-looking gingerbread. Greedy Graham had made a tottering tower of sweets with *Chocolate Hairballs*, FOAM TEETH, BELCHER-SQUELCHERS and **Blobby-Gobbers**.

129

Then there were Peter's lopsided lumpies.

And Allergic Alice's gluten-free-nut-free-sugar-free-flour-free-dairy-free-beetroot-rice-cake.

Taste-free too, thought Horrid Henry.

And a rag-tag collection of DROOPY cakes and wobbly pies.

"Wah," wailed Weepy William. "I dropped mine."

Horrid Henry and MOODY MARGARET shoved through the crowd

as the famous judge, *Cherry Berry*, stood behind the cake table.

Henry had made sure his cake was at the front.

Margaret had also made sure her cake was at the front.

The two **chocolate** sponges faced each other.

"Nah nah ne nah nah, my cake is best," jeered Margaret.

"**Nah nah ne nah nah**, my cake is best," jeered Henry.

They *glared* at each other.

Tee hee, thought Margaret.

Tee hee, thought Henry.

"Stand back from the cakes, you'll all get a chance to taste them soon," said *Cherry Berry*.

She walked around the table, eyeing the goodies. She **poked** one, **prodded** another, sniffed a third. She walked around again. And again.

Then she stopped in front of Henry and Margaret's cakes.

Henry held his breath.

Yes!

"Now, don't these SPONGE cakes look lovely," said Cherry Berry. "So attractive. So fluffy. Ooh, I do love a light sponge," she said, cutting a piece and taking a big bite.

"So SPONGY," she choked, spitting out a piece of yellow kitchen sponge. "UGGGGHHH."

RATS, thought Horrid Henry.

Cherry Berry checked the name on the flag.

"Henry's cake is disqualified."

DOUBLE RATS, thought Horrid Henry.

"Ha ha ha ha ha," screeched Moody Margaret.

"The winner is . . . Margaret."

"**YES!**" shrieked Margaret.

Aaaarrrggghhhh.

That was his cake. It was so unfair. His cake had won after all. He'd pay Margaret back—

"I'll just try a little piece before we share it with everyone," said Cherry Berry, taking a huge bite.

"**BLECCCCHHH!**" gagged Cherry, spitting it out. "Salt! Salt instead of sugar."

"What?" screamed Moody Margaret.

How was it possible that salt had been sneaked into her cake?

Unless . . . unless . . .

"You put a SPONGE in my cake," shouted Margaret.

"You put salt in my cake," shouted Henry.

Horrid Henry grabbed a pie and *hurled* it at Margaret.

Moody Margaret grabbed a cake and

hurled it at Henry.

Horrid Henry **ducked**.

The **gooey** cake landed in *Cherry Berry's* face.

"Food fight!" shrieked Rude Ralph, snatching cupcakes and throwing them.

"**FOOD FIGHT!**" screamed Greedy Graham, pitching pies into the crowd.

"Stop it! Stop it!" shouted Mum, as whipped cream **splatted** on her head.

"Stop it!" shouted Dad, as a lemon tart **splatted** on his shirt.

Cherry Berry brushed cake from

her face and pie from her hair.

"Wah," she wailed, as cake dripped down her back. "I have a soggy bottom."

She staggered over to the cake table and gripped the edge.

The table was empty except for a few grey cupcakes.

"I proclaim Peter's lopsided LUMPIES the winner," she gasped.

"Yippee," squealed Perfect Peter.

"Noooooo," howled Horrid Henry.

HORRID HENRY

KRAZY KETCHUP

"Boys," shouted Mum up the stairs. "Dinner's ready."

"Ralph! Catch."

Horrid Henry threw FLUFF PUFF, Peter's favourite plastic sheep, to Ralph.

Rude Ralph caught it, and threw it back to Henry over Peter's head.

"Give me back my sheep," said Perfect Peter.

"How much will you pay me, **Wormy Worm?**" said Horrid Henry.

"Mum!" screamed Perfect Peter.

"Henry stole FLUFF PUFF and he won't give him back. And he called me Wormy Worm."

"Tell-tale," hissed Henry.

FLUFF PUFF flew through the air, a sheep in flight, and landed **smack** on the floor.

"Henry," shouted Mum. "Say sorry for calling Peter names. And get down here **NOW**."

"Sorry I called you **Wormy Worm**," said Henry, "when I meant to call you **POOPSICLE**."

"MUUUUM!" shrieked Peter. He picked up **FLUFF PUFF** and ran downstairs.

"Boys. For the last time. Dinner's ready."

Henry and Ralph **stomped** downstairs and sat at the table.

"What's for dinner?" said Horrid Henry.

"Cauliflower cheese," said Dad.

"**ICK**," said Henry.

"**YUCK**," said Ralph rudely. "I hate cauliflower. I need **ketchup**."

"Yeah," said Horrid Henry. "Me too. **Ketchup** makes everything taste **GREAT**."

"No **ketchup** for me," said Perfect Peter. "It's much too sweet."

Mum smiled at Peter.

"It certainly is," said Mum. "**Ketchup** has lots of sugar in it."

Wow, thought **Horrid Henry**. Wow. **Ketchup** was even more **WONDERFUL** than he'd thought.

When he became a *billionaire* with his top-secret **Ketchup** recipes, and, naturally, his own brand, **Henry's Incredible Ketchup**, he'd put in loads more sugar. Then it would taste even better.

Mum reached for the sauce and

squirted
a TEENY WEENY

drop onto Henry's plate. Then she did
the same to Ralph's plate.

"That's not enough," Henry howled.
"I need **MORE**. I want **ketchup** on my
ketchup."

"Yeah," said Rude Ralph. "Gimme
more."

How could anyone eat cauliflower
unless its **HORRIBLE** white
knobbly-ness was covered in
ketchup? And beans without
ketchup? Or eggs without **ketchup?**

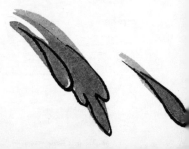

GROSS. Nothing could hide their horrible beaniness, or revolting egginess, but **ketchup** helped.

"Don't be **HORRID**, Henry," said Mum.

"But I LOVE **ketchup**," said Horrid Henry. He loved the taste of **ketchup**. He loved the smell of **ketchup**. He loved the GLUG GLUG GLUG noise **ketchup** made as it slurped out of the bottle and plopped onto his plate. There was nothing that didn't taste a million billion trillion times better covered in YUMMY SCRUMMY **Krazy Ketchup**, the world's best brand.

Every hundred years or so, when his **MEAN**, **HORRIBLE** parents took him to BRILLIANT BURGER, he'd snatch loads of their **Krazy Ketchup** sachets to stash in his bedroom, just in case the world ended or all the **Ketchup** factories burned down.

YUM. YUM. YUMMM. Krazy Ketchup. The nicest two words in the English language. (Apart from

chocolate, PIZZA, **BURGER**, **CHIPS**, **Make Your Own Hot Fudge Sundae**, and **No School Today**.)

Unfortunately, Horrid Henry's parents **HATED** ketchup. They **HATED** the taste of **ketchup**. They **HATED** the smell of **ketchup**. Most of all, they **HATED** it when Henry wanted **ketchup** at every meal.

But how else could he eat his parents' **DISGUSTING** food? One day Mum and Dad would find his *skeleton* in a corner, bony hands outstretched towards the fridge . . .

Didn't they know you could die from lack of **Ketchup?**

"My family eat everything with **Ketchup**," said Ralph. "Pasta with **Ketchup**, mashed potatoes with **Ketchup**, *ice cream* with **Ketchup**. And I always squirt my own. I'm not a baby."

"See?" said Henry.

Mum made a face.

"Everyone I know gets to squirt their own **Ketchup**," wailed Horrid

Henry. "Everyone except me. I wish Ralph's parents were mine instead of you."

Mum looked at Dad.

Dad looked at Mum.

"No one I know squirts their own," said Perfect Peter. "Little children always take too much."

Horrid Henry kicked Peter under the table.

"Mum!" squealed Peter. "Henry **kicked** me."

"Didn't."

"Did."

"It was an accident," said Horrid Henry. "I was just stretching my legs. I can't help it if yours got in the way."

"What's for *dessert*?" said Ralph rudely, pushing away his plate.

"Fruit salad," said Mum.

"**BLECCCCCH**," said Rude Ralph. "I'm not eating dinner here again."

Horrid Henry lay on his bed

reading a **Mutant Max** comic and
scoffing a few biscuits from his top-
secret tin.

Knock knock.

Henry leapt up and ran to his desk.

"I'm doing my homework," he said.

Mum and Dad peeped round the door.

"Maybe we've been too strict," said
Mum.

What? thought Henry.

"We'll try it
tomorrow and
see," said Dad.

"Try what?" said Horrid Henry, scowling. Some **YUCKY** new food? Making him do even more chores? Living without **TV?**

"Try letting you squirt your own **ketchup**," said Mum.

Henry's jaw **dropped**. Was it possible that his parents had actually listened? That for once in his life he was getting his own way? Had **aliens** taken over their bodies?

But **Horrid Henry** wasn't going to ruin everything by asking.

"**Ketchup ketchup ketchup** here

I come!" he crowed. Oh happy happy
day.

Sniff. Sniff. Sniff.

Horrid Henry stopped turning
all of Peter's sheep upside down.

What was that **YUMMY** smell?
Henry sniffed again.

CHIPS! thought Horrid Henry. He
could smell their lovely frying golden

goodness all the way upstairs.

They were actually having **CHIPS** with dinner. On the first day that the new **squirt-your-own-ketchup** rules applied.

What luck.

For once his **CHIPS** would be swimming in a **ketchup** bath. Oh yeah. And he'd be sure to steal loads of Peter's when he wasn't looking. Tee hee.

Horrid Henry dropped **FLUFF PUFF** on his head and galloped down the stairs.

Oh wow. Even better. **FISH FINGERS AND CHIPS!**

Unfortunately, Dad was sure to ruin everything and make peas too, but he could disguise their hideous green taste by drowning them in yummy, scrummy **ketchup**.

Speaking of which—

Horrid Henry looked in the fridge.

No **ketchup**.

He flung open the cupboard.

No **ketchup**.

He checked on the table, behind the toaster, and on top of the counter.

Had Mum hidden it?

Had Dad secretly **GUZZLED** it?

Had the thing **Horrid Henry** dreaded most in all the world actually happened?

Henry's blood ran cold. His heart stopped beating. His nose stopped breathing. His legs collapsed under him.

"Where's the **ketchup?**" gasped Horrid Henry. "I'll starve without it. How could we run out of **ketchup?** You said I could pour my own and now there's no **ketchup** to pour. **NOOOOOOO!**"

"Stop being **HORRID**, Henry," said Mum. "It's on the table."

"Right in front of your nose," said Dad, opening the oven and taking

out the fish fingers and chips.

Horrid Henry stopped howling and sat down in his chair.

A brown plastic bottle with a big picture of a smiling speckled tomato stood on the table.

"What's that?" said Henry suspiciously.

"**Ketchup**," said Mum.

"No it isn't," said Henry.

"It's just as tasty," said Dad.

Horrid Henry squinted at the bottle. Vegchup Tomato Ketchup, read the label.

Horrid Henry recoiled as if a poisonous hydra had just reared its nine heads.

"**ICK!**" said Henry. He made a gagging noise. "This has tomatoes in it. I want real **ketchup**. I want **Krazy Ketchup**."

"All **ketchup** has tomatoes in it," said Mum.

"No way," said Horrid Henry.

He **HATED** tomatoes. He knew it was called tomato **Ketchup** but he'd just thought it was referring to **Ketchup** being red. Not that there were actual, real tomatoes in it.

"Go ahead, try some," said Mum, serving up the chips. "You can pour your own."

Horrid Henry squirted a great big fat **BLOB** onto his pirate plate.

It wasn't a lovely, thick, red **Ketchuppy** blob. This **BLOB** was brown. Watery. Oily. It oozed on the plate.

"It looks **HORRIBLE**," screamed Henry.

"How can you tell until you try it?" said Mum.

Horrid Henry screwed up his face and took a teeny tiny taste.

BLECCCCCCCHHHH.

He spat it out.

"It's **HORRIBLE!!!** I can taste the tomatoes. And vegetables!"

"This is organic, healthy, sugar-free **ketchup**," said Mum.

"Sounds yummy," said Perfect Peter. "I can't wait to try some."

"Shut up, Peter," said Henry.

"Mum," wailed Peter. "Henry told me to shut up."

"I want **Krazy Ketchup!**" screamed Horrid Henry. "Gimme real **ketchup**."

"This is real **ketchup**," said Peter.

He reached for the bottle.

"No it isn't," shouted Henry. "Does this look like **ketchup** to you?"

Horrid Henry snatched the bottle from Peter.

Peter tried to *yank* it back.

"Henry! Peter! Stop fighting!" screamed Mum, grabbing the bottle.

"Gimme that **Ketchup**," said Dad.

Squeeze!
Splat!
Plop!
Glop!

Ketchup landed on Mum's head.

Ketchup landed on Dad's face.

Ketchup splatted on Peter's jumper and Henry's shirt.

There was **ketchup** on the floor.

There was **ketchup** on the door.

There was **ketchup** on the ceiling.

Mum, Dad, Peter and Henry were covered in **ketchup**.

"**EEEEKK**," yelled Mum.

"Take your plates and go to your rooms, both of you!" yelled Dad.

"Wah," wailed Peter.

Ketchup dribbled down Mum's face. She licked her lips.

"This tastes **HORRIBLE**," she said.

Dad wiped some **Ketchup** off his face and licked his finger.

He scowled.

"Ugh," he said. "That's **REVOLTING**."

"See?" said Horrid Henry. "Told you."

Horrid Henry sat on his bed drowning his chips in sachet after sachet of his emergency **Krazy Ketchup** stash. He knew he'd been right to stockpile it.

Ah! **Krazy Ketchup** and chips. Was there anything better to eat in the whole wide world?

And oh yes. He had the feeling that Krazy Ketchup would be back in his kitchen very soon.

HORRID HENRY

BANK ROBBER

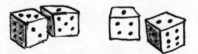

"I want the skull!"
"I want the skull!"
"I want the skull!" said
Horrid Henry, glaring.

"You had it last time, Henry," said
Perfect Peter. "I never get it."

"Did not."

"Did too."

"I'm the guest so I get the skull,"
said Moody Margaret, **SNATCHING**
it from the box. "You can have the
claw."

"**NOOOOOOOO!**" wailed Henry. "The
skull is my lucky piece."

Margaret looked smug. "You know I'm going to win, Henry, 'cause I always do. So ha ha ha."

"Wanna bet?" muttered Horrid Henry.

The good news was that Horrid Henry was playing GOTCHA, the world's best board game. Horrid Henry loved GOTCHA. You rolled the dice and travelled round the board, collecting TREASURE, buying dragon lairs and praying you didn't land in your enemies' lairs or in the Dungeon.

The bad news was that Horrid

Henry was having to play GOTCHA
with his **worm** toad crybaby brother.

The worst news was that Moody
Margaret, the world's **biggest**
cheater, was playing with them.
Margaret's mum was out for the
afternoon, and had dumped Margaret
at Henry's. Why oh why did she have
to play at his house? Why couldn't
her mum just dump her in the bin
where she belonged?

Unfortunately, the last time they'd played GOTCHA, Margaret had won. The last two, three, four and five times they'd played, Margaret had won. Margaret was a demon GOTCHA player.

Well, not any longer.

This time, Henry was determined to beat her. Horrid Henry HATED losing. By HOOK or by CROOK, he would triumph. Moody Margaret had beaten him at GOTCHA for the very last time.

"Who'll be banker?" said Perfect Peter.

"Me," said Margaret.

"Me," said Henry. Being in charge
of all the game's TREASURE was
an excellent way of topping up your
coffers when none of the other
players was looking.

"I'm the guest so I'm banker," said
Margaret. "You can be the *dragon*
keeper."

Horrid Henry's hand itched to *yank* Margaret's hair. But then Margaret would **SCREAM** and **SCREAM** and Mum would send Henry to his room and confiscate GOTCHA until Henry was old and bald and dead.

"Touch any TREASURE that isn't yours, and you're *dragon* food," hissed Henry.

"Steal any *dragon* eggs that aren't yours and you're toast," hissed Margaret.

"If you're banker and Henry's the *dragon* keeper, what am I?" said

Perfect Peter.

"A **TOAD**," said Henry. "And count yourself lucky."

Horrid Henry snatched the dice. "I'll go first." The player who went first always had the best chance of buying up the best **dragon** lairs like **Eerie Eyrie** and **Hideous Hellmouth**.

"No," said Margaret, "I'll go first."

"I'm the youngest, I should go first," said Peter.

"**ME!**" said Margaret, snatching the dice. "I'm the guest."

"**Me!**" said Henry, snatching them back.

"Me!" said Peter.

"**MUM!**" screamed Henry and Peter.

Mum ran in. "You haven't even started playing and already you're fighting," said Mum.

"It's my turn to go first!" wailed Henry, Margaret and Peter.

"The rules say to roll the dice and whoever gets the highest number goes first," said Mum. "End of story." She left, closing the door behind her.

Henry rolled. Four. Not good.

"Peter's knee touched mine when I rolled the dice," protested Henry. "I get another turn."

"No you don't," said Margaret.

"Muuum! Henry's cheating!" shrieked Peter.

"If I get called one more time," screamed Mum from upstairs, "I will throw that game in the bin."

EEEEK.

Margaret rolled. Three.

"You *breathed* on me," hissed Margaret.

"Did not," said Henry.

"Did too," said Margaret. "I get another go."

"No way," said Henry.

Peter picked up the dice.

"Low roll, low roll, low roll," chanted Henry.

"Stop it, Henry," said Peter.

"Low roll, low roll, low roll," chanted Henry louder.

Peter rolled an eleven.

"Yippee, I go first," trilled Peter.

Henry glared at him.

Perfect Peter took a deep breath, and rolled the dice to start the game.

Five. A Fate square.

Perfect Peter moved his **gargoyle** to the Fate square and picked up a Fate card. Would it tell him to claim a **TREASURE** hoard, or send him to the **Dungeon?** He squinted at it.

"The og . . . the ogr . . . I can't read

it," he said. "The words are too hard for me."

Henry snatched the card. It read:

THE OGRES MAKE YOU KING FOR A DAY. COLLECT 20 RUBIES FROM THE OTHER PLAYERS.

"The Ogres make you king for a day. Give twenty rubies to the player on your left," read Henry. "And that's me, so pay up."

Perfect Peter handed Henry twenty rubies.

TEE HEE, thought Horrid Henry.

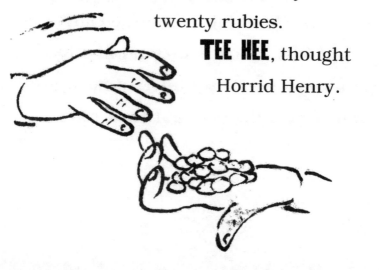

"I think you read that Fate card wrong, Henry," said Moody Margaret grimly.

Uh oh. If Margaret read Peter the card, he was **DEAD**. Mum would make them stop playing, and Henry would get into trouble. **BIG BIG TROUBLE.**

"Didn't," said Henry.

"Did," said Margaret. "I'm telling on you."

Horrid Henry looked at the card again. "Whoops. Silly me. I read it too fast," said Henry. "It says, give twenty rubies to all the other players."

"Thought so," said Moody Margaret.

Perfect Peter rolled the dice. Nine! Oh no, that took Peter straight to Eerie Eyrie, Henry's favourite lair. Now Peter could buy it. Everyone always landed on it and had to pay ransom or get eaten. RATS, RATS, RATS.

"1, 2, 3, 4, 5, 6, 7, 8, 9, look, Henry, I've landed on Eerie Eyrie and no one owns it yet," said Peter.

"Don't buy it," said Henry. "It's the WORST lair on the board. No one ever lands on it. You'd just be wasting your money."

"Oh," said Peter. He looked
doubtful. "But . . . but . . ." said Peter.

"Save your money for when you
land in other people's lairs," said
Henry. "That's what I'd do."

"Okay," said Peter, "I'm not buying."
TEE HEE.

Henry rolled. Six. Yes! He landed
on **Eerie Eyrie**. "I'm buying it!"
crowed Henry.

"But Henry," said Peter, "you just told me not to buy it."

"You shouldn't listen to me," said Henry.

"MUM!" wailed Peter.

Soon Henry owned Eerie Eyrie, Gryphon Gulch and CREEPY HOLLOW, but he was dangerously low on treasure. Margaret owned ROCKY RAVINE, VULTURE VALLEY and Hideous Hellmouth. Margaret kept her TREASURE in her treasure pouch, so it was impossible to see how much

money she had, but Henry guessed she was also low.

Peter owned **DEMON DEN** and one *dragon* egg.

Margaret was stuck in the Dungeon. Yippee! This meant if Henry landed on one of her lairs he'd be safe. Horrid Henry rolled, and landed on **VULTURE VALLEY**, guarded by a baby dragon.

"**GOTCHA!**" shrieked Margaret. "Gimme twenty-five rubies."

"You're in the Dungeon, you can't collect ransom," said Henry. "**NAH NAH NE NAH NAH!**"

"Can!"

"Can't!"

"That's how we play in my house," said Margaret.

"In case you hadn't noticed, we're not at your house," said Henry.

"But I'm the guest," said Margaret. "Gimme my money!"

"No!" shouted Henry. "You can't just make up rules."

"The rules say . . ." began Perfect Peter.

"SHUT UP, PETER!" screamed Henry and Margaret.

"I'm not paying," said Henry.

Margaret glowered. "I'll get you for this, Henry," she hissed.

It was Peter's turn. Henry had just upgraded his baby dragon guarding Eerie Eyrie to a big, **huge, fire-breathing, slavering monster dragon**.

Peter was only five squares away.
If Peter landed there, he'd be out of
the game.

"Land! Land! Land! Land! Land!"
chanted Henry. "Yum yum yum, my
dragon is just waiting to eat you up."

"Stop it, Henry," said Peter. He
rolled. Five.

"GOTCHA!" shouted Horrid Henry.
"I own Eerie Eyrie! You've landed in
my lair, pay up! That's a hundred
rubies."

"I don't have enough money,"
wailed Perfect Peter.

Horrid Henry drew his finger across his throat.

"You're **DEAD MEAT**, worm," he chortled.

Perfect Peter burst into tears and ran out of the room.

"Waaaaaaahhhhh," he wailed. "I lost!"

Horrid Henry *glared* at Moody Margaret.

Moody Margaret *glared* at **Horrid Henry**.

"You're next to be eaten," snarled Margaret.

"You're next," snarled Henry.

Henry peeked under the GOTCHA board where his TREASURE was hidden. Oh no. Not again. He'd spent so much on dragons he was down to his last few rubies. If he landed on any of Margaret's lairs, he'd be wiped out. He had to get MORE TREASURE. He had to. Why oh why had he let Margaret be banker?

His situation was desperate. Peter was easy to steal money from, but Margaret's EAGLE eyes never missed a trick. What to do, what to do? He had to get more treasure, he had to.

And then suddenly **Horrid Henry** had a brilliant, SPECTACULAR idea. It was so brilliant that Henry couldn't believe he'd never thought of it before. It was **DANGEROUS**. It was **risky**. But what choice did he have?

"I need the loo," said Henry.

"Hurry up," said Margaret, scowling.

Horrid Henry dashed to the downstairs loo . . . and sneaked straight out of the back door. Then he jumped over the garden wall and crept into Margaret's house.

Quickly he ran to her sitting room and scanned her games cupboard. Aha! There was Margaret's GOTCHA.

Horrid Henry stuffed his pockets with TREASURE. He stuffed more under his shirt and in his socks.

"Is that you, my little sugarplum?" came a voice from upstairs. "Maggie Moo-Moo?"

Henry froze. Margaret's mum was home.

"Maggie Plumpykins," cooed her mum, coming down the stairs. "Is that you-oooo?"

"NO," squeaked Henry. "I MEAN, YES," he squawked. "GOT TO GO BACK TO HENRY'S, 'bye!"

And **Horrid Henry** ran for his life.

"You took a long time," said Margaret.

Henry hugged his stomach.

"Upset tummy," he lied. Oh boy was

he brilliant. Now, with loads of CASH which he would slip under the board, he was sure to win.

Henry picked up the dice and handed them to Margaret.

"Your turn," said Henry.

Henry's hungry dragon stood waiting six places away in **Goblin Gorge**.

Roll a six, roll a six, roll a six, prayed **Horrid Henry**.

Not a six, not a six, not a six, prayed Moody Margaret.

Margaret rolled. Four. She moved her skull to the **Haunted Forest**.

"Your turn," said Margaret.

Henry rolled a three. Oh no. He'd landed on *Hideous Hellmouth*, where Margaret's giant dragon loomed.

"Yes!" squealed Margaret. "GOTCHA! You're **DEAD!** Ha ha hahaha, I won!" Moody Margaret leapt to her feet and did a victory dance, whooping and cheering.

Horrid Henry *smiled* at her.

"Oh dear," said Horrid Henry. "Oh dearie, dearie me. Looks like I'm dragon food — **NOT!**"

"What do you mean, not?" said Margaret. "You're **DEAD MEAT**, you can't pay me."

"Not so fast," said Horrid Henry. With a *flourish* he reached under the board and pulled out a wodge of **TREASURE**.

"Let me see, one hundred rubies, is it?" said Henry, counting off a pile of coins.

Margaret's mouth **dropped** open.

"How did you . . . what . . . how . . . huh?" she spluttered.

Henry shrugged modestly. "Some of us know how to play this game," he said. "Now roll."

Moody Margaret rolled and landed on a Fate square.

Go straight to **Eerie Eyrie**, read the card.

"**GOTCHA!**" shrieked Horrid Henry. He'd won!! Margaret didn't have enough money to stop being eaten. She was **DEAD**. She was **doomed**.

"I won! I won! You can't pay me, **NAH NAH NE NAH NAH**," shrieked Horrid Henry, leaping up and doing

a victory dance. "I am the GOTCHA king!"

"Says who?" said Moody Margaret, pulling a handful of TREASURE from her pouch.

Huh?

"You STOLE that money!" spluttered Henry. "You STOLE the bank's money. YOU BIG FAT CHEATER."

"Didn't."

"Did."

"CHEATER!" howled Moody Margaret.

"CHEATER!" howled Horrid Henry.

Moody Margaret grabbed the board

200

and *hurled* it to the floor.

"I won," said Horrid Henry.

"Did not."

"Did too, Maggie Moo-Moo."

"Don't call me that," said Margaret, glaring.

"Call you what, Moo-Moo?"

"I challenge you to a rematch," said Moody Margaret.

"You're on," said Horrid Henry.

HORRID HENRY

MiDSUMMER MADNESS

Turn the page for lots of fun games and activities!

Code Crackers

THIS SUMMER IT'S WAR! MOODY MARGARET'S SECRET CLUB KEEPS INFILTRATING THE PURPLE HAND GANG'S MESSAGES. THAT'S WHY HENRY HAS DEVELOPED A CODE FOR ALL MEMBERS TO USE.

A = @			J = -			S = ‡
B = +			K = ^			T = °
C = !			L = £			U = ø
D = *			M = \			V = »
E = ?			N = /			W = ~
F = $			O = .			X = ®
G = &			P = %			Y = ¿
H = >			Q = ×			Z = ɢ
I = <			R =)			

CAN YOU WORK OUT THE SECRET MESSAGE?

~@°?)   +@££../   @°°@!^
_ _ _ _ _   _ _ _ _ _ _ _   _ _ _ _ _ _

./   °>?   ‡?!)?°   !£ø+
_ _   _ _ _   _ _ _ _ _ _   _ _ _ _

./   ~?*/?‡*@¿
_ _   _ _ _ _ _ _ _ _ _

HA! HENRY THINKS HE'S SO CLEVER BUT MARGARET HAS INVENTED HER OWN SUPER-SECRET WAY OF PASSING MESSAGES.

WHO IS THE SECRET CLUB'S LATEST PRANK TARGET? CROSS OUT ALL THE LETTERS THAT APPEAR MORE THAN ONCE.

BBOORKKLLMMAJJFFEELGGWWPQQZZHNNMM

THE TARGET IS:

_____

Summer Crossword

HENRY HAS **LOTS** PLANNED FOR THIS SUMMER. CAN
YOU WORK OUT SOME OF THE THINGS HE'LL DO?

ACROSS

2. EAT LOTS OF THIS COLD DESSERT
4. HENRY'S BIRTHDAY MONTH
6. BUILD THIS AT THE BEACH
8. RIDE THIS TO RALPH'S HOUSE
9. DO THIS AT A POOL

DOWN

1. ESSENTIALS FOR A WATER FIGHT
3. A TRICK TO PLAY ON PETER
5. WEAR THESE WHEN IT IS SUNNY
6. MUM MAKES ME SIT IN THE…
7. WHEN THE WEATHER DOES THIS, I CAN WATCH TV

Running Race

HENRY AND AEROBIC AL ARE RACING TO THE SWEET SHOP – BUT THEY HAVE FOUND SWEETS ON THE WAY! WHO HAS THE FEWEST SWEETS ON THEIR PATH?

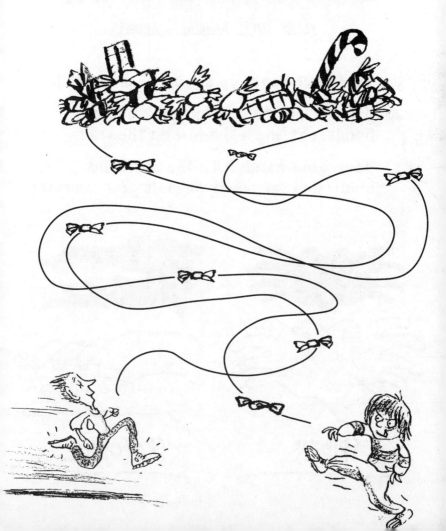

Shadow Puppets

MOODY MARGARET HAS THE SECRET CLUB OVER FOR A SLEEPOVER. THEIR HEADQUARTERS ARE THE PERFECT PLACE FOR SHADOW HAND PUPPETS! WHY DON'T YOU TRY TO MAKE THESE ANIMAL SHADOWS?

1. Hold your hands up against a plain wall

2. Ask a friend to point a torch at your hands, casting a shadow on the wall

3. Move your hands into the positions below and see which animals you can make

SPIDER   CROCODILE

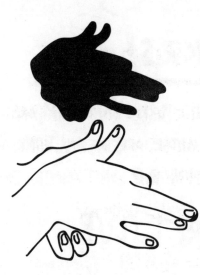

DOG

COCKEREL

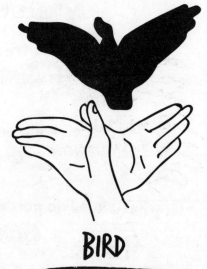

RABBIT

BIRD

JOKES!

THE SECRET CLUB AND THE PURPLE HAND GANG ARE IN A COMEDY BATTLE! WHOSE JOKES DO YOU THINK ARE FUNNIEST?

THE SECRET CLUB

Q: what do you call a fake noodle?
A: An impasta

Q: How do you make a tissue dance?
A: Put a little boogie in it!

Q: what does a tree do when it is ready to go home?   **A: It leaves!**

Q: what do you get when you cross a snowman with a vampire?   **A: Frostbite.**

Q: what sound do porcupines make when they kiss?
A: Ouch!

THE PURPLE HAND GANG

Q: Why are pirates called pirates?

A: 'Cause they arrrrr.

Q: How does the ocean say hello?

A: It waves.

Q: What is a witch's favourite subject at school? A: Spelling!

Q: Why did the picture go to prison?

A: Because it was framed.

Q: What do you call a dinosaur that is sleeping? A: A dino-snore!

Car Games

WHY DO PARENTS ALWAYS WANT TO TAKE YOU PLACES IN THE SUMMER HOLIDAYS? HENRY MAKES BORING CAR JOURNEYS MUCH MORE FUN BY PLAYING THESE GAMES!

1. NOW!

Take turns to pick a point in the distance like a bridge or a sign — then close your eyes and when you think the car has reached that point say "Now!" (Henry likes to give bonus points if you shout "Now!" loud enough that someone in another car looks over.)

2. TWENTY QUESTIONS

Think of a person, place or thing. The next player has twenty yes or no questions to guess what it is! (If you're stuck for things to think of, Henry suggests TV, sweets, money and comic books.)

3. WHO LIVES HERE?

Take turns making up life stories about the people who live in the houses you pass. (And don't forget to include vampires, witches and werewolves!)

4. NAME A PLACE

One person names a place and the next person has to say a place that starts with the last letter of the previous place — see how many you can list before someone gets stuck! (And all of these countries, cities and towns sound way more interesting than wherever Henry's parents are taking him.)

Riddles

PETER HAS BEEN TELLING RIDDLES ALL SUMMER AND HENRY HAS HAD ENOUGH! HE'S DECIDED TO WRITE HIS OWN TO SHOW PETER WHO'S BEST.

PETER'S RIDDLES

What has a face and two hands, but no arms or legs?

A CLOCK

What five-letter word becomes shorter when you add two letters to it?

SHORT

What gets wetter as it dries? **A TOWEL**

What word begins and ends with an 'e' but only has one letter?

ENVELOPE

HENRY'S RIDDLES

How many letters are there in the English alphabet?

18!
There are 3 in 'the', 7 in 'English'
and 8 in 'alphabet'

Which month has 28 days?

ALL OF THEM, ALTHOUGH SOME ALSO
HAVE A FEW MORE

Railway crossing without any cars. Can you spell
that without any Rs? **T-H-A-T**

What is brown and sticky? **A STICK**

How many apples grow on a tree?

ALL APPLES GROW ON TREES

Holiday Packing

HENRY IS STRUGGLING TO FIT IN ALL THE CRISPS,
COMIC BOOKS AND OTHER TRAVEL ESSENTIALS INTO HIS
SUITCASE...DRAW WHAT ELSE YOU THINK HE WOULD PACK.

Sandcastles

HENRY AND PETER ARE HAVING A SANDCASTLE
COMPETITION – CAN YOU HELP DECORATE THEM?

Fun Facts

CLEVER CLARE ISN'T GOING TO WASTE HER SUMMER LIKE OTHER CHILDREN — SHE'S LEARNING AS MUCH AS SHE CAN. HERE ARE SOME OF HER FAVOURITE FACTS:

1. The world's oldest piece of chewing gum is over 9,000 years old

2. Bolts of lightning can shoot out of an active volcano

3. A crocodile can't poke out its tongue

4. Ketchup was used as medicine in the 1930s

5. Gorillas burp when they are happy

6. Pirates wore earrings because they thought it improved eyesight

7. Sometimes waterfalls go up instead of down

8. You are shorter in the evening than in the morning

9. It's impossible to sneeze with your eyes open

10. Elephants are the only mammals that can't jump

Campsite Chaos

HENRY'S PARENTS HAVE DRAGGED HIM CAMPING AND NOW HE CAN'T REMEMBER WHICH TENT IS HIS! IT'S THE ONLY ONE THAT DOESN'T MATCH ANOTHER TENT – CAN YOU FIND THE TENT THAT'S DIFFERENT FROM THE REST?

Who Am I?

DO YOU KNOW YOUR ANXIOUS ANDREWS FROM YOUR BRAINY BRIANS? CAN YOU WORK OUT WHO EACH OF THESE CHARACTERS ARE?

1. My brother is very mean and always calls me a worm. I'm the leader of the Best Boys Club.

2. I'm the fastest boy at school and love sports!

3. I dunno.

4. I am a teacher and Henry's class is the worst I have ever taught – and Henry is by far the worst child!

5. Henry and Peter are my cousins. They're very poor and don't get nearly as many presents as I do.

6. La la la –I love singing!

7. I'm the best girl in the world – I'm the smartest, the fastest and the most talented. The Secret Club is way better than the Purple Hand Gang!

8. I love Henwy. I want to mawwy him.

9. Meow.

10. I love being a teacher – my class are so … lovely!

Answers

Code Crackers

~@°?)   +@££../   @°°@!^
Water   balloon   attack

./   °>?   ‡?!)?°   !£ø+
on   the   Secret   Club

./   ~?*/?‡*@¿
on   Wednesday

THE TARGET IS:

RALPH

Summer Crossword

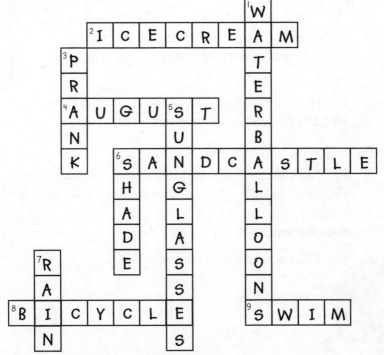

Running Race

Aerobic Al has fewer sweets on his path!

Campsite Chaos

The odd one out is …

Who am I?

1 Perfect Peter
2 Aerobic Al
3 Beefy Bert
4 Miss Battle-Axe
5 Stuck-up Steve

6 Singing Soraya
7 Moody Margaret
8 Lisping Lily
9 Fluffy
10 Miss Lovely

COLLECT ALL THE
HORRID HENRY STORYBOOKS!